The Watcher

Story by Brenda Silsbe   Illustrations by Alice Priestley

Annick Press Ltd.
Toronto • New York

©1995 Brenda Silsbe (text)
©1995 Alice Priestley (art)
Designed by Sheryl Shapiro.

Second printing, October 1995

Annick Press Ltd.

Annick Press gratefully acknowledges the support of the Canada
Council and the Ontario Arts Council.

Canadian Cataloguing in Publication Data
Silsbe, Brenda
  The watcher

ISBN 1-55037-385-4 (bound) ISBN 1-55037-384-6 (pbk.)

I. Priestley, Alice. II. Title.

PS8587.I268W3 1994 jC813'.54 C94-932297-0
PZ7.S55Wa 1994

The art in this book was rendered in pencil crayon.
The text was typeset in Century Oldstyle.

Distributed in Canada by:
Firefly Books Ltd.
250 Sparks Avenue
Willowdale, ON
M2H 2S4

Published in the U.S.A. by Annick Press (U.S.) Ltd.
Distributed in the U.S.A. by:
Firefly Books (U.S.) Inc.
P.O. Box 1338
Ellicott Station
Buffalo, NY 14205

∞ Printed on acid-free paper.

Printed and bound in Canada by
Friesens, Altona, Manitoba.

To my father, Ray Taft.
B.S.

To my brother, Michael.
A.P.

George was a watcher. He watched TV. He watched cars, trucks and big machines. George watched clouds in summer...and snow falling in winter. George loved to watch shoppers at the mall and birds at the bird feeder.

Most of the kids at school were players, not watchers. They climbed and ran and played with balls. They sang and swung and slid down halls.

"George doesn't do anything!" they said. "George doesn't like skating, and he never plays soccer. He won't even throw snowballs." His brothers were worried about George.

But George did do something.
He watched.

Every day, when George came home from school, he told his mother everything he had seen.

George told his mother what his teacher wore. He told her what the class had learned, what was new and what the other kids did, like Dan getting a nosebleed when he walked into a flagpole.

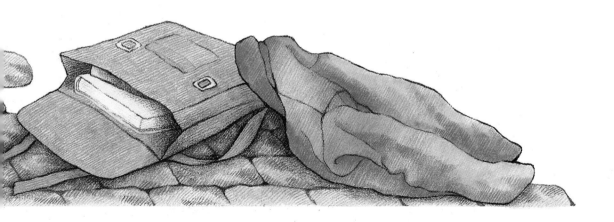

George's mother thought she was in heaven: whenever she asked George's brothers what they did in school, they always said, "Nothing."

But George saw everything.

One Monday at noon, all the kids at school were gathered in the cafeteria.

George sat quietly eating his lunch, watching the helpers dish out macaroni and hot dogs, watching orange juice rising up through drinking straws, watching the kids trade their desserts and watching the rain stream down the windows.

Suddenly, from across the room, George noticed Sarah, a girl from his class. She was clutching her throat and staring wildly at the kids around her.

"Sarah!" yelled George.

The cafeteria grew deathly
quiet. Everyone had become
watchers—even the supervisor.
They sat frozen, staring at Sarah.

George saw the school nurse walking in the hall. George sprang out of his seat, jumped over two tables and shouted, in his loudest voice, "Miss Clayton!"

The nurse stopped and looked at George.

"Sarah's choking!" yelled George. He pointed at her.

Miss Clayton ran to Sarah. She knew just what to do.

When Sarah was breathing again, Miss Clayton led her away.

Everyone looked at George.

"It's a good thing you were here, George," said Dan.

"I saw a safety show on TV," said George. "It said to stay calm and take charge. So I did."

The kids all slapped George on the back and said, "Great!" and "Excellent!"

George watched the kids go back to their seats.

From that time on, the other kids asked George many questions. George found lost things, he helped solve problems and he had a lot of interesting things to say in Science and Socials.

"It's good to have a watcher in the class," said the teacher. But George didn't hear him: crows were fighting over a sandwich on the playground, a new moon was rising in the sky, Spike's nose was running and the class hamster was trying to escape from its cage.

George was watching.

Other titles by the author:

Just One More Colour
Winning the Girl of the Sea
The Bears We Know *(Annikin edition only)*